MARVIN HAMLISCH

Marvin Makes Music

ILLUSTRATED BY

JIM MADSEN

Dial Books for Young Readers *An Imprint of Penguin Group (USA) Inc.*

*For my parents, Lilly and Max Hamlisch; my sister, Theresa; my beloved Terre;
my first piano teacher, Mr. Edgar Roberts; and The Juilliard School of Music.
They all helped me to hear the music in my mind.*
—M.H.

For Holly, my amazing wife.
—J.M.

· ·

ACKNOWLEDGMENTS

Thank you to my literary agent Anna Olswanger, my editor Steve Meltzer, and
Stephanie Owens Lurie. Thank you to Judith Clurman and her Essential Voices USA,
and to Jonah Kernis for the recording.

I hope this book will inspire kids everywhere to hear the music around them.
—Marvin Hamlisch

· ·

DIAL BOOKS FOR YOUNG READERS
A division of Penguin Young Readers Group

Published by the Penguin Group
Penguin Group (USA) Inc., 375 Hudson Street, New York, New York 10014, U.S.A. • Penguin Group (Canada), 90 Eglinton Avenue East,
Suite 700, Toronto, Ontario M4P 2Y3, Canada (a division of Pearson Penguin Canada Inc.) • Penguin Books Ltd, 80 Strand, London
WC2R 0RL, England • Penguin Ireland, 25 St Stephen's Green, Dublin 2, Ireland (a division of Penguin Books Ltd) Penguin Group
(Australia), 250 Camberwell Road, Camberwell, Victoria 3124, Australia (a division of Pearson Australia Group Pty Ltd) • Penguin Books
India Pvt Ltd, 11 Community Centre, Panchsheel Park, New Delhi–110 017, India • Penguin Group (NZ), 67 Apollo Drive, Rosedale,
Auckland 0632, New Zealand (a division of Pearson New Zealand Ltd) • Penguin Books (South Africa) (Pty) Ltd, 24 Sturdee Avenue,
Rosebank, Johannesburg 2196, South Africa • Penguin Books Ltd, Registered Offices: 80 Strand, London WC2R 0RL, England

Library of Congress Cataloging-in-Publication Data
Hamlisch, Marvin.
Marvin makes music/Marvin Hamlisch; illustrated by Jim Madsen.—1st ed.
p. cm.
Summary: Young Marvin loves music and playing the piano but does not like practicing pieces by people named Ludwig
or Wolfgang, until he receives valuable advice from his father on the day of a big audition.
ISBN 978-0-8037-3730-3 (hardcover)
1. Hamlisch, Marvin—Childhood and youth—Juvenile fiction.
2. Hamlisch, Marvin—Childhood and youth—Fiction. [1. Pianists—Fiction.
2. Composers—Fiction.] I. Madsen, Jim, date, ill. II. Title.
PZ7.H1834Mar 2012 [E]—dc23 2011052317

Published in the United States by Dial Books for Young Readers, a division of Penguin Young Readers Group
345 Hudson Street, New York, New York 10014 • www.penguin.com/youngreaders

Designed by Jason Henry
Manufactured in China • First Edition
1 3 5 7 9 10 8 6 4 2

$\mathscr{M}$arvin was born to play music. He felt more comfortable on a piano bench than anywhere else. The piano was his best friend.

Wherever he went, he heard music. In the park, other people watched the birds. Marvin listened to their songs. On the street, when car horns blared, Marvin knew what notes they were honking. When he played baseball, he thought about making melodies, not home runs.

At home he played the latest songs he'd heard on the radio, and he loved composing his own tunes. Music flowed into his ears and out of his fingers.

B ut playing piano wasn't always fun.

"Practice, Marvin, practice," his father reminded him.

All that practice was too much. Marvin didn't like the old music his piano teacher made him play. And all those exercises just made him sleepy. He tried all kinds of excuses: He forgot to clean his room. He was starving. He had to go to the bathroom. (Marvin used that one so much his mother wanted to call the doctor.)

He became pretty good at finding hiding places just so he wouldn't have to practice.

Whenever someone came over to his house, his father would say, "Listen to our Marvin play." The audience could be anyone—a neighbor, an aunt, or even the mail carrier.

Marvin didn't like that. Performing for other people gave him butterflies in the belly.

"My poor little boy," his mother would say.

"He's okay, Mama," said his father. "All he needs to do is practice."

Everyone liked Marvin's playing, but he wondered why he had to play music by composers with funny names, like Wolfgang and Ludwig. Why couldn't he just play his own songs and have fun?

Marvin loved music. It could take him on fantastic journeys. He'd close his eyes and daydream that he was the conductor for a very important orchestra. Best of all, they were playing his songs.

One day Marvin's father sat down next to him.

"Your piano teacher and I both think you're ready to enroll in one of the best music schools in the city. It won't be easy. You'll have to play in front of three judges—without missing a note."

That was harder than playing for neighbors. Just thinking about it brought back the butterflies.

Marvin's father started telling everyone that Marvin was going to audition for the important school. They were all so impressed. Marvin was scared that this was a really big deal.

*M*arvin was nervous on the morning of the audition. What if he made a mistake? He didn't want to disappoint everyone.

His mother kissed him and gave him a surprise: "Sweetheart, I bought you a brand-new suit for your special day."

It was Marvin's first suit. He was so excited. He felt all grown up—a suit just like his father wore.

But after a few minutes the wool in the suit made his legs itchy, and all he wanted to do was scratch.

What would he do? He couldn't play the piano when he was all itchy and scratchy.

"Don't worry, Marvin," said his mother. "Wear your soft pajamas underneath and you won't feel itchy."

That was much better, but Marvin felt a little silly wearing his orange bear pajamas underneath his suit.

arvin and his father arrived for the audition early and decided to explore the school. They peeked into classrooms, read notices on the bulletin boards, and watched students go from class to class. But still they were early.

"Tell you what, Marvin," said his father, "let's go up on the roof. It's such a nice day."

That sounded like fun to Marvin. He even climbed the stairs two at a time.

It was a clear day, and the sky was a beautiful blue. His father pointed out famous buildings around the city while Marvin watched the clouds pass by. One of the fluffy clouds reminded him of a soft lullaby.

His father showed him how the people on the street below looked like ants, but to Marvin they looked like musical notes. That made him start humming a little tune.

Marvin closed his eyes and listened to all the sounds around him. He wished he could play his piano right now. It would be a City Symphony. . . .

Marvin opened his eyes and looked at his father.

"Daddy, the music I love is the music I hear in my head, not that old music I have to keep practicing."

Marvin's father smiled. "Marvin, I know this is hard for you. I know you like to write songs, but the better you learn the piano, the better you can play them. Someday you will be playing not just for relatives, but for the whole world." Then he kissed his son on the forehead.

Marvin smiled, too. Being on the roof and talking to his father made him feel better. He could face the judges and play his best now.

They headed for the door to go back downstairs.

It was locked!

"Help! Help!" Marvin pounded on the dirty roof door with his fists.

No one answered.

His father leaned over the edge of the roof and shouted down to the street, "We're locked out!"

Finally someone heard them and came to open the door.

$\mathcal{M}$arvin arrived at his audition twenty-five minutes late. His hair was uncombed, his hands were covered with soot, and his new suit was all messy.

"You're late, young man," one judge said sternly. "You might as well begin."

Marvin walked over and sat down at the piano.

He slowly raised his fingers. He thought about the music and what his father had told him, and just like that, everything changed. He was back with his best friend, the piano, and nothing else mattered. Marvin forgot about the judges and let the music sweep him along. It carried him far, far away from that windowless room, back up to the rooftop . . . and beyond.

It was only when the last note had faded away that Marvin remembered where he was and what he was doing there.

He looked toward the judges. They seemed happy. They were smiling, but then two of them started to laugh.

What was so funny? And why were the judges pointing at Marvin's feet?

Marvin looked down. The little orange bears were sticking out from the bottom of his suit pants. Even he had to laugh.

Marvin passed the audition and was invited to attend the school. His mother and father were so proud, they read his acceptance letter to anyone who would listen. Marvin didn't feel that much different, though. He still had to practice and sometimes he still became nervous when performing for people. But that didn't matter so much anymore. Because he knew one day he would be playing music, his music, and that . . .

. . . would be magic.

The Music in My Mind

Music by Marvin Hamlisch ♫ Lyrics by Rupert Holmes

The sound of falling rain,
Or lemonade that's stirred,
The whistle of a train,
The whistling of a bird.
To some it's only noise,
But every sound I've heard
Seems sure like,
Much more like
A song.

The music in my mind belongs to me.
Ev'ry note I hear rings true.
And soon the world will find these sounds
   and songs to be worth singing:
Like summer rains and wooden spoons,
And passing trains and popped balloons,
And every sound from far and near,
It won't be long before you hear them, too.

A siren passing by,
A plane that's flying low,
Potatoes as they fry,
A nose you gotta blow,
The shouts of girls and boys
Out sledding in the snow . . .
An earful, as cheerful as a song!

The music in my mind belongs to me.
Ev'ry note I hear rings true.
And soon the world will find these sounds
   and songs to be worth singing:

Of soaring airplanes in the skies,
A siren's blare or sizzling fries,
A honking horn, a honking nose,
Or popping corn or winter snows,
And summer rains and wooden spoons,
And passing trains and popped balloons,
And every sound from far and near,
It won't be long before you hear
The music in our mind belongs to us.
Every note we sing rings true.
If days are gray we'll find bright sounds
   in songs and just keep singing . . .
A lion's roar, a cricket's chirp,
A father's snore, a baby's burp,
The ticking sounds of tapping feet,
A subway pounds beneath the street,
Or soaring airplanes in the skies,
A siren's blare and sizzling fries,
A honking horn, a honking nose,
Or popping corn or winter snows,
And summer rains and wooden spoons,
And passing trains and popped balloons,
And every sound of any kind,
It won't be long before you find . . .
The music in your mind!